An Adams' Wood Mystery

WHO ATE THE CAKE?

Follow the clues and find the answer

Written by Stewart Cowley
Illustrated by Susi Adams

DERRYDALE BOOKS
NEW YORK

Published 1986 by Derrydale Books,
distributed by Crown Publishers, Inc.

Produced for Derrydale Books by
Victoria House Publishing Ltd.
4/5 Lower Borough Walls
Bath BA1 1QR, England

Printed in Belgium

Welcome to Adams' Wood

"Hello, I'm Holmes Mouse, the great detective!"

"And I'm Watson Mouse, his best friend!"

This is a story about a birthday party. There were games and presents and special birthday treats. But someone stole a piece of the birthday cake! Can you help us find out who it was?

Read the story and look at the pictures carefully to find the clues. We will be looking for clues, too—watch out for us.

If you don't solve the mystery, we've put together all the evidence in one big picture near the end of the book ... and if you still don't know who ate the cake, we may have found the answer for you.

"Here's a letter for you!" called Peter Pigeon the
Postman. "Oh, thank you," said Mr. Frog. "It's an
invitation to Robbie's birthday party! I hope there's lots
of birthday cake."
"You'll have to be quick," said Peter. "Everyone's
invited."

Mrs. Raccoon welcomed each guest as they arrived and gave them a paper party hat to wear. "Hurry along!" she called. "There are games and presents for all of you—and a delicious birthday cake!"

All the children had a chance at the grab bag, only this time it was a 'grab barrel.' The barrel was full of presents. "Just one each!" laughed Mr. Raccoon. Some naughty children tried to take two!

Billy got a trumpet. "Listen to me," he said to Robbie and began to play. "What a horrible noise," said Robbie. "Come on, I'm hungry. Let's see if it's time for the cake!"

Robbie's presents were piled high for everyone to see. "Come on, Robbie!" his friends called. "Open your presents. We want to see what you've gotten before we have the cake." But Robbie was nowhere to be found.

"Well, I don't know," said Mr. Rabbit.
"We can't start eating without Robbie.
Where is he? I better go and look for
him." And off he went to ask Mrs.
Hedgehog if she had seen him.

"Quickly now!
It's not just
Robbie
who's hungry!"

Mrs. Hedgehog had the candles for Robbie's birthday cake. "He must be here somewhere," she said. "He helped Miss Mouse carry the birthday cake to the table. Now where is it? I must put these candles on it before we can start."

Just then they heard a shout. It was Miss Mouse. "Oh no!" she cried. "Look at my lovely cake. Someone has eaten part of it. Robbie will be upset! Who could have done such a thing?"

Mr. Rabbit asked Mrs. Duck. But she was playing Blind
Man's Buff—so she couldn't have seen who did it.

Billy was playing Pin a Tail on the Donkey. "I can't see anything," he said.

"Is everybody busy playing games?"

All the baby mice were playing musical chairs. "What cake?" they asked, giggling.

"Whoever ate the cake has been this way!"

Sammy Squirrel had been playing Hide-and-Seek with Robbie, but now Sammy couldn't find him anywhere. When he sat down for a rest, he quickly jumped up. "Oooh!" he said. "What have I sat on? It looks like frosting."

"Look over here," called Mrs. Squirrel. "There's a big pile of crumbs in the grass. How could they have gotten there?"

Mr. Fox came over to take a look.
"What's this?" he cried. And there,
nearby, was a special paper party hat
hanging on a twig. "I think I know who
stole the cake, don't you?"

"We know who did it.
Do you? Turn the
page and see
who's hiding."

"I think I've had enough now," mumbled Robbie
through a mouthful of crumbs. "Anybody want a piece
of birthday cake? It's very good!"